Five reasons why we think you'll love this book!

Winnie and Wilbur

THE BIG BAD ROBOT

Why not be just like Vinnie and make a junk model robot?

Contains robot rabbits, robot frogs, and robot ducks!

In this story Wilbur is a real hero!

There is so much to spot in every picture.

You can take the Winnie and Wilbur challenge: how many light bulbs can you find?

Freya

Anushka

Maggie

Bailey

Johannes

Molly

Ashley

Amber

Jun-Yeong

Pablo

Matilda

Marwin

Hasan

Rebecca

Thank you to all these schools for helping
with the endpapers:

St Barnabas Primary School, Oxford; St Ebbe's
Primary School, Oxford; Marcham Primary School,
Abingdon; St Michael's C.E. Aided Primary School,
Oxford; St Bede's RC Primary School, Jarrow;
The Western Academy, Beijing, China; John King
School, Pinxton; Neston Primary School, Neston;
Star of the Sea RC Primary School, Whitley
Bay; José Jorge Letria Primary School, Cascais,
Portugal; Dunmore Primary School, Abingdon;
Özel Bahçeşehir İlköğretim Okulu, Istanbul,
Turkey; the International School of Amsterdam,
the Netherlands; Princethorpe Infant School,
Birmingham.

For Sam and Natalie—V.T.

For Kate and Captain Jack—K.P.

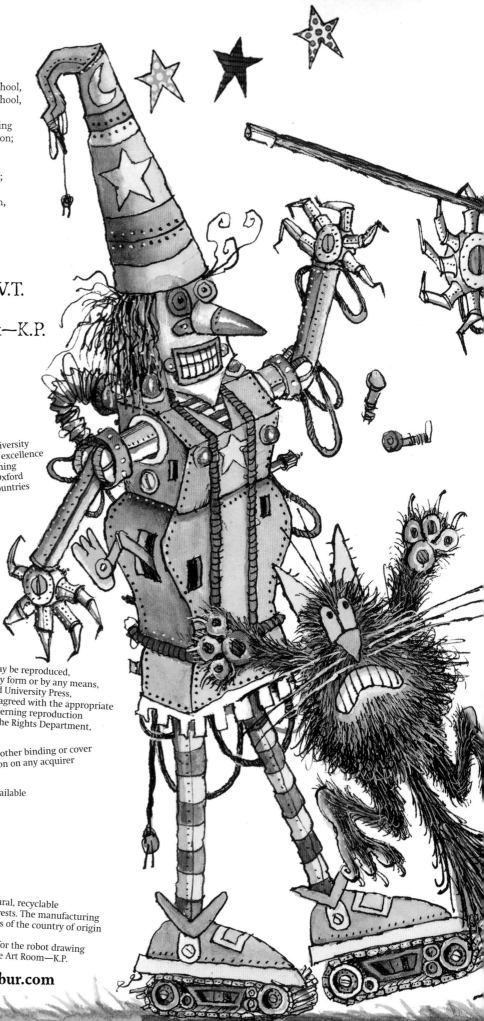

OXFORD
UNIVERSITY PRESS

Great Clarendon Street, Oxford OX2 6DP

Oxford University Press is a department of the University
of Oxford. It furthers the University's objective of excellence
in research, scholarship, and education by publishing
worldwide. Oxford is a registered trade mark of Oxford
University Press in the UK and in certain other countries

Text copyright © Valerie Thomas 2014
Illustrations copyright © Korky Paul 2014, 2016
The moral rights of the author and artist
have been asserted

Database right Oxford University Press (maker)

First published as *Winnie's Big Bad Robot* in 2014

This edition first published in 2016

British Library Cataloguing in Publication Data available

ISBN: 978-0-19-276676-2

10 9 8 7 6 5 4 3 2 1
Printed in China

Paper used in the production of this book is a natural, recyclable
product made from wood grown in sustainable forests. The manufacturing
process conforms to the environmental regulations of the country of origin

Thanks to Anderson, Wilder, and Schuyler Daffey for the robot drawing
in Winnie's kitchen. This helped raise funds for the Art Room—K.P.

www.winnieandwilbur.com

VALERIE THOMAS AND KORKY PAUL

Winnie AND Wilbur

THE BIG BAD ROBOT

OXFORD
UNIVERSITY PRESS

Every Wednesday afternoon Winnie the Witch and her big black cat Wilbur went to art classes in the library.

They learned how to paint
and draw, knit and sew,
make pots and posters,
and lots of other things.
Winnie the Witch really
enjoyed *all* of the classes.

Wilbur enjoyed *some* of them.

This Wednesday they were making models.
Winnie decided to make a bear.

She chose a cardboard box for the head.

She glued on the eyes, nose, and mouth.

Then she made the body,

arms,

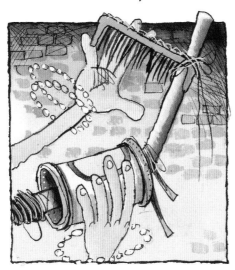

and legs.

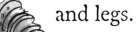

It looked good. The teacher liked it too.

'That's a lovely robot you've made, Winnie,' she said. Winnie was cross. *A robot?*

But when she looked at it carefully, it did look a bit like a robot. Everybody admired it.

Winnie sat the robot on her broomstick.
Then Winnie, Wilbur, and the robot flew home.

Winnie stood the robot on the kitchen table.
'It's a pity it's not a real robot,' she said.

Then Winnie had an idea
She picked up her magic
wand, shouted,

'Abracadabra!'

. . . and there in the kitchen was a real robot.
'Beep, beep, beep,' said the robot.
Its eyes flashed red and green.

Winnie was delighted.
'Isn't this a lovely robot, Wilbur?' Winnie said.

Wilbur didn't think so.
The robot walked over to
Wilbur and pulled his tail.
'Yeeoww!' cried Wilbur.

'Naughty robot!' Winnie said.
'You mustn't pull poor Wilbur's tail!'

The robot looked at Winnie.
Then it leaned over and pinched her nose.
'Oww!' said Winnie. 'That hurt.
I've made a bad robot, Wilbur.
I'll change it back into a model.'

Winnie went to pick up her magic wand.
But the robot was too fast for her.

It grabbed
Winnie's wand,

walked up the wall,

across the ceiling,

and then out of the window.

'Oh no!' shouted Winnie.
'My wand still has the robot spell on it, Wilbur.
We have to get it back.'

Winnie and Wilbur tiptoed
out of the front door.
They hid behind the tallest tree.

The big bad robot
was waving Winnie's wand.

Two robot frogs jumped into the pond.
Three robot ducks flew across the sky.
The robot waved the wand again and
four robot rabbits hopped across the grass.

Then the robot waved the wand
at Winnie's front door . . .

and there was an enormous robot house.

Winnie waited until the robot walked past the tree.

She jumped out,

'Blithering broomsticks!' Winnie whispered. 'My lovely house is a robot house! We have to get my wand back, Wilbur.'

and Winnie the Witch was Winnie the Robot.

Oh no!

Winnie the Robot walked round and round
the garden.
'Beep, beep, beep,' she said.

'Meeoow!' said Wilbur.
He didn't like Winnie the Robot.
He wanted Winnie the Witch back again.
He would have to get Winnie's wand.

But how?

Wilbur had an excellent idea.

He grabbed a creeper . . .

swung out over the big
bad robot, and snatched
Winnie's wand.

Then he swung across to Winnie the Robot,

and dropped the wand into her hand.

Winnie the Robot waved the wand again and again, and shouted,

'Abra-beep-beep-cadabra ...'

Two frogs jumped into the pond,
three ducks flew up into the sky,
four rabbits hopped across the grass,
the robot house was Winnie's house,
Winnie the Robot was Winnie the Witch,
and instead of a big bad robot there was
a little pile of junk.

Winnie the Witch flopped down
into her deckchair.
Wilbur curled up in her lap.

'Thank you, Wilbur,' Winnie said.
'I am very lucky to have such a clever cat.'
'Purr, purr, purr,' said Wilbur.

Bethany

Katia

Eun-Jae

Kathleen

Ji-Eun

Jenny

Sara

Fraser

Ka Keung

Selin

Selin

Olivia

Siyabend

Kieran

A note for grown-ups

Oxford Owl is a FREE and easy-to-use website packed with support and advice about everything to do with reading.

Informative videos

Hints, tips and fun activities

Top tips from top writers for reading with your child

Help with choosing picture books

For this expert advice and much, much more about how children learn to read and how to keep them reading ...

LOOK
for Oxford Owl
www.oxfordowl.co.uk